This book belongs to

....

This is a Parragon Publishing book
First published in 2007

Parragon Publishing
Queen Street House
4 Queen Street
Bath BA1 1HE, UK

Copyright © Parragon Books Ltd 2007

ISBN 978-1-4054-9107-5
Printed in China

Alice in Wonderland

Written by Lewis Carroll
Retold by Rachel Elliot
Illustrated by Shelagh McNicholas

Alice was sitting by her sister on the bank,
when a White Rabbit with pink eyes ran past.
"Oh dear! I shall be late!" said the Rabbit.
Alice followed it and found herself falling down
a deep well.

Down, down, down.
"I must be getting near
the center of the Earth,"
thought Alice.
Down, down, down. Alice was
starting to doze off when THUMP!
She landed on a heap of dry leaves,
and the fall was over.

Alice was standing in a
long hall, lined with doors.
There was a little glass
table with a tiny golden
key on it. Alice tried the
key in all the doors, but it
wouldn't open any of them.

Then she saw a tiny door behind a low curtain.
The golden key opened it! The door led into a
beautiful garden, but Alice could not even get
her head through the doorway.

She went back to the table and found a little bottle labeled "DRINK ME." When she tried it, she started to shrink!
Alice was now just the right size for going through the door. But the golden key was on the table, and she couldn't reach it.

Then she saw a very small cake, with "EAT ME" written on it in raisins. Alice decided to try it!

"Curiouser and curiouser!" she said.

The cake made her grow so big that her head hit the ceiling! Poor Alice cried until there was a large pool of tears all around her. Suddenly the White Rabbit ran past with a pair of white gloves and a fan. When he saw Alice, he dropped them and scurried away. Alice picked them up and fanned herself. The fan made her shrink!

Alice's foot slipped and SPLASH!
She was up to her chin in the pool of tears.

"I wish I hadn't cried so much!" said Alice.
Lots of birds and animals had fallen into the water. There
were a Duck and a Dodo, a Parrot and an Eaglet, a mouse
and several other curious creatures. Together, they all
swam to the shore.

The birds and animals were dripping wet.

"I think that a Caucus race would get us dry," said the Dodo.

"What is a Caucus race?" said Alice.

"The best way to explain it is to do it," said the Dodo. It marked out a racecourse in a circle. There was no "Get ready. Get set. Go!" but they started running when they liked, and stopped when they liked. When they were quite dry, the race was over.

Everyone crowded around, asking who had won.

"Everybody has won, and all must have prizes," said the Dodo. Alice found some candies in her pocket and handed them around as prizes. Then she tried to tell her new friends about her cat, Dinah. But she scared all the birds and little animals! They ran away, and poor Alice was alone again.

Alice walked on and came to a thick wood. She saw a Caterpillar sitting on top of a large mushroom and smoking a hookah.

"Who are you?" said the Caterpillar sleepily.

"I don't know" said Alice. "I think I've been changed several times."

"Explain yourself!" said the Caterpillar.

"I can't explain myself," said Alice. "I'm not myself. I don't stay the same size for ten minutes together!"

The Caterpillar crawled away from the mushroom.

"One side will make you grow taller, and the other side will make you grow shorter," it said.

"One side of what? The other side of what?" Alice asked.

"Of the mushroom," said the Caterpillar.

Alice stretched her arms around the mushroom and broke off a bit with each hand. She nibbled at the pieces. The right-hand piece made her grow smaller, and the left-hand piece made her grow larger.

Alice came to a tiny house. She used the right-hand piece to grow smaller, and went inside.

"Speak roughly to your little boy,
And beat him when he sneezes:
He only does it to annoy,
Because he knows it teases."

A Duchess was sitting on a stool, sneezing a lullaby to a howling, sneezing baby. The cook was stirring a cauldron of soup, and the air was full of pepper. The only ones not sneezing were the cook and a large, grinning cat.

"Why does your cat grin like that?" said Alice.

"It's a Cheshire cat," snapped the Duchess, flinging the baby at Alice.

"I must get ready to play croquet with the Queen."

Alice caught the baby and walked outside.

The baby gave a loud grunt. It had a very turned-up nose, just like a snout. It grunted again. There was no mistake about it—it was a pig. Alice put the pig down and it trotted away. She saw the Cheshire Cat sitting in a tree.

"Who else lives around here?" she asked.

"A Hatter and a March Hare," the Cat said. "They're both mad."

"I don't want to be among mad people," Alice remarked.

"You can't help that," said the Cat. "We're all mad here."

Then it vanished, starting with the tail, and ending with the grin.

Alice found the March Hare's house. She joined the March Hare,
the Hatter, and a sleepy Dormouse at a huge table.

"Why is a raven like a writing desk?" asked
the Hatter.

"I give up," Alice said. "What's the answer?"

"I haven't the slightest idea," said the Hatter.

"I want a clean cup."

They all moved one place on. Alice took
the place of the March Hare, who had
just spilled the milk jug into his plate.

"Have some more tea," said the March Hare.

"I've had nothing yet," said Alice, "so I can't have more!"

"Once there were three little sisters," yawned the Dormouse, "and they lived at the bottom of a well—"

"What did they live on?" she asked.

"Treacle," said the Dormouse.

"I don't think—" began Alice.

"Then you shouldn't talk," said the Hatter.

Alice thought they were all very rude. She got up and walked off. "I'll never go there again!" said Alice. "It's the stupidest tea party I was ever at!"

At last Alice found the beautiful garden. The King and Queen of
Hearts came toward her, with soldiers, courtiers, and the White Rabbit.

"Can you play croquet?" roared the Queen.

"Yes!" Alice cried.

It was a very strange croquet ground. The balls were live hedgehogs, the mallets were live flamingos, and the soldiers doubled over to make the arches. Soon the Queen was in a furious temper, shouting "Off with his head!" or "Off with her head!" about once a minute.

Then Alice noticed a grin appearing in the air.

"It's the Cheshire Cat!" said Alice.

"How are you getting on?" it asked.

"I don't think they play fairly," Alice began. Then the Queen saw the Cat. "Off with its head!" she shouted. But, before the executioner could do anything, the Cat began fading away. Soon it had completely disappeared.

The Queen sent Alice to meet the Gryphon and the melancholy Mock Turtle.

"Once I was a real Turtle," he said sadly. "I went to school in the sea." "What did you learn?" asked Alice. "Reeling and Writhing, of course," he replied, "and then Ambition, Distraction, Uglification, and Derision."

The Mock Turtle and the Gryphon showed Alice how to dance the Lobster Quadrille.

Then the Mock Turtle sang a song. Suddenly they heard someone shout,
  "The trial's beginning!"
  "Come on!" cried the Gryphon.

"Beautiful Soup, so rich and green,
        Waiting in a hot tureen!
Who for such dainties would not stoop?
Soup of the evening, beautiful Soup!
Soup of the evening, beautiful Soup!
        Beau–ootiful Soo–oop!
        Beau–ootiful Soo–oop!
    Soo–oop of the e–e–evening,
      Beautiful, beautiful Soup!"

The King and Queen of Hearts were on their thrones in court, and the Knave was under arrest. The White Rabbit read the accusation:

"The Queen of Hearts, she made some tarts,
All on a summer day:
The Knave of Hearts, he stole those tarts,
And took them quite away!"

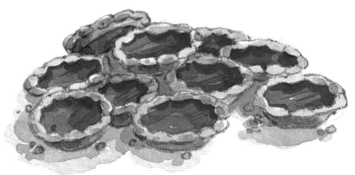

Just then, Alice had a very strange feeling. She was starting to grow larger again.

"Call the first witness!" said the King. The first witness was the Hatter.

"I'm a poor man," he trembled, "and I hadn't begun my tea—and what with the bread-and-butter getting so thin—and the twinkling of the tea—"

"Next witness!" cried the King.

The next witness was the Duchess's cook. Alice guessed who it was, even before she saw her, by the way everyone started sneezing.

"Give your evidence," said the King.

"Shan't," said the cook.

"Next witness!" the King cried.

The White Rabbit read out the name "Alice!"

"What do you know about this business?" the King asked Alice.

"Nothing," said Alice.

"That's very important," the King told the jury.

"Unimportant, your Majesty means," said the White Rabbit.

"Unimportant, of course," the King said quickly. He scribbled in his notebook and read out, "Rule Forty-two. All persons more than a mile high to leave the court." Everybody looked at Alice.

"I'm not a mile high," said Alice. "Besides, that's not a proper rule. You invented it just now."

"It's the oldest rule in the book," said the King.

"Then it ought to be Number One," said Alice.

The King shut his notebook.

"Consider your verdict," he said to the jury.

"No!" said the Queen. "Sentence first—verdict afterward."

"Stuff and nonsense!" said Alice loudly.

"Off with her head!" the Queen shouted.

"Who cares for you?" said Alice. "You're nothing but a pack of cards!"

The whole pack rose up into the air, and came flying at her!

Alice tried to beat the cards off, and found herself lying on the bank with her head in her sister's lap. Some leaves had landed on her face.

"Wake up, Alice!" said her sister. "What a long sleep you've had!"

"I've had such a curious dream!" said Alice.

And as the sun set, Alice told her sister about the things she had done, and the strange creatures she had met, and all her curious, marvelous Adventures in Wonderland.